All Things Dark
And Dangerous

A.S.Chambers

Acknowledgements

Many thanks to all the great people I have met over the years and who have bought my books. Thank you so much for all your feedback, kind words and creepily wonderful stalking techniques.

Also by A.S.Chambers

Ebook short stories.
High Moon - 2013
Girls Just Wanna Have Fun – 2013
Needs Must - 2019

Novellas.
Songbird – 2019
Bobby Normal and The Eternal Talisman – 2021
Bobby Normal and the Virtuous Man – 2021
Bobby Normal and the Children of Cain – 2022
Bobby Normal and the Children of Cain – 2022
Bobby Normal and The Fallen – 2023
Bobby Normal and the Black Dragon – 2024
Child of Light – Due 2024
Child of Fire – Due 2025

Omnibuses.
Children of Cain - 2019
Macabre Collection: Volume One – 2022
Macabre Collection: Volume Two – 2023
Sam Spallucci Omnibus: Volume One – 2022
Sam Spallucci Omnibus: Volume Two – 2024
The Adventures of Bobby Normal – 2024

Contents

First Hunt – Now

The black four by four drew to a halt on the sparsely gravelled path. A pair of legs swung out from a rear door into the cool, moonlit night. Their owner drew in a deep, refreshing breath of highland air and smiled to himself. It was a curious sensation as he performed it just for pleasure not for the act of respiration.

He had no need for that now.

He was, for all intents and purposes, dead.

"You okay?"

Dave Nichols, former proprietor of a small comic book shop in a city in the North West of England, turned to the woman (if you could call her that) who had taken his mortal life. "Never been better," he smiled. "Never been better."

Nightingale closed the passenger's door with a solid click and made her way round to her newly born off-spring. She took his hand in hers and smiled up into his eyes. "Good. I'm glad."

"Everything feels so different," the newborn whispered into the night. "I know that's cliché but..."

"That's okay. I was totally the same. There's so

1

much for you to learn. That's why we've come here."

There was a solid clunk as the driver's door shut. "So hadn't we better get on with it then?" came a clipped, masculine voice. "We only have a few hours until sunrise."

"Patience, Marcus." Nightingale turned to her long-standing companion. "We'll go and settle ourselves down in the cabin. We'll be perfectly safe in there when the sun comes up." With that, she led her companion and her child up the gravel path towards the old cabin that stood overlooking the sea from the cliffside. After just a few steps she and the older of the two males stopped dead in their tracks.

"What is it?" Dave asked.

Nightingale flicked a sidewards glance to Marcus and he was suddenly a blur of colour as he streaked up the rest of the path to the cabin and in through the door.

"Nightingale..."

She held a hand up to silence her child as her sharp eyes scanned the ground between them and the cabin. A few seconds later Marcus opened the door again and walked at a more sedate pace back towards the car. "It's all clear," he said.

Nightingale frowned. "But they've definitely been here." It was a statement, not a question.

Marcus nodded slowly. "There's something else, too."

Nightingale cocked her head to one side in a question but her progeny cut in before Marcus could answer. "Who? Who's been here?"

The young mother looked her child straight in the eye. "Constructs."

Dave looked on feeling somewhat helpless as the other two vampires circled the immediate area around the cabin. Every now and then one or both of them would stand still, scent the air then crouch to examine the rough ground. He had no idea what was going on. It was obviously something of importance and danger, but as to its exact nature...

So he stood propped against the four by four and waited until the others had completed their recce before making their way back to him. "What's going on?" he asked.

"This is supposed to be a safe house," Nightingale explained. "We often bring new-borns here to help them through their initial transition and to train them. It is known to no-one outside of our community."

"And yet Constructs have been here," Marcus growled, his eyes flitting from spot to spot as if seeing things that were not there, "and there's been fighting."

Dave ran his fingers through his sandy-coloured hair. "Okay. So I'm guessing this is bad?"

Nightingale nodded. "Very."

"And there's more." Marcus began pointing to various spots around the cabin. "There's been some sort of battle here. There is dried blood on the ground and bullet cases. There was a firefight."

Dave frowned. "Bullets? So they weren't after a vampire then?"

Nightingale smiled. "Good logic. The blood is neither Construct nor Vampire. Come and see this." She led her child over to the edge of the cliff. "See here where the stone has crumbled? There are splatter patterns around the damaged stone. Bend down close and smell it."

Dave did as instructed. He knelt on one knee and lowered his nose to the ground. He caught a symphony of fragrances: grass, soil, sea, rock and... and... He gasped as the sweetest aroma he had ever tasted hit his brain. "Wow! What is that? I feel like I'm smelling a rainbow!"

Marcus turned to Nightingale and lifted a sardonic eyebrow. Nightingale smiled softly. "We don't know. It's definitely not Construct. You remember what that tasted like?"

Dave nodded, recalling a few nights ago back in Lancaster when his new instincts had taken over and he had attacked a woman who, at the time, he had not consciously known to be a Construct. "It was dark, artificial – as if someone had made something to appear like human blood but had not quite got it right. There was also that grainy aftertaste."

"Correct." Nightingale crouched down next to him. "Quite unlike your friend's blood."

Dave shuddered at that thought. He had been forced to drink the blood of Sam Spallucci, the man who had been taking care of him. If he had not done so he would have remained incomplete. "His blood was so...alive."

"Exactly. Sam is a living creature. Constructs are just what their name suggests. They have been made to look like humans. This, however," she traced a finger along the dark stain on the rocks, "is something completely different. Someone very special was here."

Dave straightened up and ran his fingers through his mop of hair. "This is so confusing. There's so much to learn. Tell me more. Tell me about the Constructs."

"They are soulless demons." Marcus' deep voice cut across the still night. "They have no conscience or

4

ounce of goodness in them. They are creations, simulacra intended to infiltrate humanity and sit there, waiting."

"Waiting? What for?"

Nightingale stood and idly brushed some dirt off her trousers. "We're not entirely sure. Part of the problem is that most of them do not know what they are. They are sleeper agents of some sort, programmed to wake at a specific moment or cue. They can spend years thinking they are human. They may have mundane, day-to-day jobs or they may have positions of power. Wherever they are we have to track them down and kill them."

"Why?"

Nightingale answered with deep sadness. "Because if we don't, then they will eradicate our kind. As soon as they awaken then their true nature becomes manifest and they will hunt down the nearest Child of Cain and slaughter him or her no matter what the consequence. We have lost many to them."

The three vampires started to walk towards the cabin as the youngster mulled this over.

"So, if they are sleepers, then who programmed them?"

"Kanor." The one word from Marcus' lips was spat like a curse. "Until you had your vision, we had no name for him, but now we know our enemy."

Dave stopped and stared down at his feet. "And I will die in his presence."

He felt a cool hand brush his cheek. "We cannot change our future, my child, but we can do what we must for that which we hold to be of utmost importance."

He lifted his eyes and looked into Nightingale's sad orbs. "Find the Eternals. Protect the Twins. Await the Divergence."

Nightingale nodded. "That's right. That is what the very first of our kind was instructed to do, and we must follow his example."

They resumed their walk to the cabin. "By our very first do you mean Cain?"

Marcus opened the old, wooden door and they entered the shack. It was dark and smelt musty. There were, however, obvious signs that it had been recently inhabited: a dead fire in the hearth, blankets on the small bed and food left discarded on the table. The older of the two male vampires picked up the stale bread and sniffed it with disgust. "Cain was visited by a stranger just after he slew his brother, Abel. He was full to the brim with remorse and regret at his rash action. The stranger gave him a chance for redemption. He turned him into a vampire and told him to go out and spread his kind amongst the human world with those three instructions. So that is what we have done since the dawn of civilisation." He tossed the bread with precision into a bucket that sat next to the fire. A small cloud of ashes plumed up in its wake.

"So," Dave asked as he settled into a creaking, wooden chair that felt in danger of imminent collapse, "who was the stranger?"

Nightingale perched in front of him on the table and smiled. "He was an angel. We have angelic blood coursing through our veins."

It was starting to be a night of revelations: creatures fashioned and sent by some big bad to wipe out vampires; the father of all vampires was an angel. If he had been a smoker then Dave would have been puffing his way through a pack of twenty.

"Are there any more little secrets you'd like to tell me about?"

His mother smiled lovingly at him. "Oh, there are plenty, my child, but right now we have a more pressing matter." She rose and made her way over to a grubby window. Closing her eyes, she inhaled deeply before turning to her companion. "Two?" she asked.

"That was my count," Marcus agreed. "Over in the woods. I would imagine they have seen us and are waiting to see where we go so that they can follow us."

Nightingale nodded. "Very well." Turning to Dave, she grinned. "Well, it appears tonight you shall have your first practical lesson.

"You're going to learn how to hunt."

A short while later, Dave was creeping through the undergrowth of a nearby copse with Nightingale at his side. He was trying his best to move stealthily but, to his hypersensitive hearing, every step sounded like a thunderclap and every broken stick a gunshot. "Surely they'll hear us?" he asked in a voice that sounded to him like a tornado ripping through a densely populated city.

Nightingale slowly shook her head, not for once taking her eyes off the shadows that danced between the trees in the moonlight. "We are superior in every way. We move faster and with greater stealth. We have heightened senses. They are no different to humans except for their physical makeup. They will not hear us unless we make a drastic mistake."

"Physical makeup?"

"Constructs are not creatures of flesh and blood," the older vampire explained. "They are made from a clay-like substance that allows them to resemble humans and blend into society. Be careful, though. They are killers and can adapt their form accordingly."

7

Dave ran his fingers through his hair again. He felt less than reassured. "So whereabouts is Marcus now?"

"Close your eyes and inhale slowly. See what your senses tell you."

The young vampire did as he was instructed. He lightly closed his eyelids and drew a long, deep breath in through his nose. There were the fresh green leaves, the grass, the soil. Those scents were all-pervading as if he was enveloped in a blanket woven by Mother Nature herself. Then there was an acrid tang that reminded him of cities. Diesel? Yes, it was the car in which they had driven to this place. Curiously, he could pinpoint it way back behind them, which told him that the cabin lay a small distance to their rear. He concentrated on what was passing over the cells in his nose and picked up two more distinct smells. One was crisp and clean, fresh with the scent of expensive cologne. That was Marcus. He let his brain play with the strength and intensity that it recognised as the norm for when the older vampire was standing in his presence and that, along with his skin feeling the slight breeze of the night gave him an answer. He was just about to say that their companion was in the region of fifty metres away when the second scent muscled its way into his senses.

Dave grunted with revulsion. It was a scent that was wrong. It smelt human but had an earthy undercurrent that told of dark, dank places next to foetid swamps. He almost gagged as he snapped his eyes open and rubbed his mouth on the back of his hand.

Nightingale was looking straight at him. "Good. You smelt them didn't you?"

"Yes, they are very close. Marcus is a bit further away."

"He will come at them from the other side as planned," she explained. "Lead on. Take me to them." She gestured with her arm deeper into the woods.

As the two vampires walked slowly through the dense undergrowth, a stray thought crossed Dave's mind. "Nightingale?"

"Yes, my child."

"Do we have a leader? Some sort of King Vampire?"

He expected an amused chuckle, but instead there was a sorrowful sigh. "That is an awkward question to answer at the moment."

"Why?"

"Well," Nightingale paused as she obviously sought out the simplest explanation, "we do have a structure for leadership. To simplify it somewhat, our leader has always been the oldest vampire in the bloodline closest to the original source. So, in the beginning it would have been Cain. Cain then had children. When he died, his oldest took on the role of leader. When he died then his child took over and so on. If the vampire died without leaving an heir then their sibling would become king or queen. It is very similar to human monarchy."

"Okay, so who is in charge now, then?"

Nightingale stopped and leaned against a tree. "The situation is somewhat complex."

Dave frowned. "How?"

"The head of the line at the moment never wanted to be King. To make it worse, he..." She momentarily examined the earth at her feet before looking back up. "He suffered a great loss that broke his mind. He is not stable."

"So you have no leader at the moment?"

9

"We have a Regent."

"And who is that?"

Silence hung between them in the woods until Nightingale volunteered, "That would be me. And now we are going to change the subject. We have work to do."

Dave gave a quick nod. He guessed it was best not to annoy the new boss. "So what's the plan?"

"You go in there quickly and you kill them both."

Dave felt his stomach clench with sudden apprehension. "Me?" he hissed in the dark.

There was no reply. He turned to where Nightingale had been standing and saw empty woods. He was on his own.

Nightingale looked down from the canopy. She could easily make out her child down below. He was frantically turning this way and that in blind panic, all recent lessons apparently forgotten, as he tried to locate her. Not once did he look up. She smiled softly. This would be fun to watch. As light as her namesake she skipped from branch to branch hardly causing a stir. The reddening leaves of autumn did not rustle and within a few seconds she was nestled at the top of a large tree by a clearing.

There they were.

She inhaled slowly. The air reeked of them: their foulness, their wrongness. She swallowed hungrily as she yearned to leap down and dispatch them, drain them of their life force, but that was not to be tonight. Not unless something went drastically wrong.

Tonight belonged to her offspring just as the night of her first hunt had belonged to her so many years ago. Her brow creased with amusement. Who was she kidding? She was under two hundred years old, a mere child in vampire years. There were others out there who were in their thousands; ones who had seen ancient empires rise and fall.

Yet she was their superior. She was their ruler through right of birth. This was not a path she desired but such was her fate. It had fallen in her lap and she had to deal with it, just as, one day, she would have to deal with her older brother.

However, that was a thought for another time. Right now, she had to watch and wait.

"Okay, okay," Dave muttered under his breath, "I can do this. I've done it before without even thinking. It can't be that hard, can it?" He thought back to the night in Lancaster. Instinct had taken over automatically. He had sensed the Construct and just reacted. His muscles had responded without any prompting and he had zeroed in on her, grasping her tight and plunging his teeth in.

Rhythmically, he rocked back on the balls of his feet, concentrating on the two presences in the clearing ahead. He focussed all his senses on them and felt his body prepare for the charge. His stomach growled in hunger. That was good. That was good. He was ready. Yes, he was.

He swung his arms back and forth by his sides just as he used to in gym class when he was preparing to sprint down the running track. Back and forth they swung, long pendulums building up potential power ready to propel him after his prey. He closed his eyes, breathed deep, placed a foot forward ready to run and...

Came to a sudden stop after one foot fall.

What was he doing?

This was insane!

They had not done anything to him. How could he take their lives? He had been repulsed after his attack on the girl in the Sugar House. It had made him physically sick. When he had found her corpse outside, exsanguinated and dumped, it had screamed against all his moral values.

It had been wrong.

He ran his fingers through his sandy hair in frustration. Oh, this was not good. What was he to do?

He had an idea. He would go and watch them first, creep up to the edge of the clearing and spy on them. Surely if they were evil incarnate then he would be able to see so and then he would attack.

Yes. That was what he would do. That was a plan.

With a large helping of stealth and a good dose of trepidation, Dave carefully picked his way to the edge of the clearing. Gradually, he began to make out darkness rather than trees as he approached the edge of the wooded area. His ears picked out two voices as his prey talked to each other. He listened in. It was hardly the machinations of evil geniuses. They were discussing television. One was berating the judges of Strictly Come Dancing for letting some overweight TV chef take part even though, in the speaker's honest opinion, he was completely talentless. His companion berated him and told him not to be so heartless. He told him that it was only a television show, not the end of the world. They then went on to discuss the X Factor and Simon Cowell.

Dave frowned. They could not be evil creatures, surely? Did Nightingale have it wrong? Was she mistaken? Had his own senses deceived him earlier? There was only one way to find out.

He stepped out into the clearing.

"Hello there!" he called out.

What on Earth was he doing? Nightingale almost broke the branch of the tree as her grip increased exponentially at her sudden anxiety. Her eyes must surely be deceiving her. Dave was actually walking over to the Constructs and talking to them.

Actually talking to them!

She looked over to the other side of the clearing. She could just make out the broken outline of Marcus partially obscured by undergrowth. He had her child covered, but all the same, this was going horribly wrong.

What was he thinking? Part of her was screaming that she ought to jump down and intervene, slay the creatures where they stood, but that would defeat the object of the exercise. This was Dave's night. She had to leave him be.

And other vampires wondered why she had taken so long to decide to become a mother...

The two men turned and faced Dave as he stepped out of the tree line. He saw looks of worry pass between their confused faces.

Okay, he could do this. "No need to panic. I was just passing by and overheard you."

One of the strangers turned towards him. "In a forest? In the middle of the night?"

Dave winced. Yes, it did sound odd now he thought about it. "I...like night walks," he smiled amiably. "They're so refreshing."

Both of the strangers were now standing up in the middle of the clearing providing him with a perfect view of them. One was in his forties, fairly stout with grey hair and the other was a few years younger, slim and blonde. Both of them had a backpack on the ground at their feet. They looked for all intents and purposes like a couple of walkers. Certainly not like homicidal maniacs.

If anyone filled that role right now, it was the crazy guy who had just walked out of the woods. Dave sighed. This was not going to plan. "Listen, to be honest, I'm kind of lost. I think I took the wrong path awhile back. Have you guys got a map?"

The younger one looked to the older who raised an eyebrow and shrugged. "Sure," said blondie. "It's in my pack. Come over here and I'll dig it out for you." He bent over and started to unfasten his bag.

Dave walked over to the two men and presented his friendliest smile. "Well, this is very kind of you." As he turned to watch the younger man rummage in his bag, he heard a noise that sounded like mud sliding off a wellington boot. His instincts screamed and he swivelled to see the older man bearing down on him. His attacker's hand had transformed into a long, dark stake. It was being thrust towards his chest when there was a blur and suddenly the man's head was missing. The decapitated body carried forward with its momentum pushing it on and toppled over at Dave's feet. He saw Marcus coming to a stop a couple of metres away with the man's head in his hands.

The young vampire felt a change in the air around him and, without thinking, leapt at the blonde man who was now charging towards Marcus. Dave flew through the air and clung onto his target's back, gripping his prey's right hand as it slipped and slid into a long, hard weapon akin to that of his late companion's. The Construct discharged a rough grunt as it was manhandled to the floor. Rage and hunger welled up inside the hunter who drew his head back, exposing his sharp teeth before plunging them down into his victim's neck.

The vampire drank heavily, imbibing furiously on the thick liquid that passed for the creature's blood. As he drank, he felt the writhing and wriggling of his prey lessen and its physical form weakened under his weight. He gripped the creature tight in his grasp and, as its skin desiccated, he felt its stake-hand snap off between his tightly clasping fingers.

Then there was nothing. The husk of a body could give him no more.

It was empty and Dave's immediate hunger had been sated.

He pushed off from the corpse and cried into the still night air as fire rocketed around his veins and capillaries. Kneeling in the grass he panted heavily as his dead heart pumped invigorated lifeblood around his body. He realised that his eyes were closed and when he opened them he saw Marcus draining the decapitated remains of the other Construct. He had sunk his teeth deep into one of its wrists and was sucking every drop of remnant life from its withering form.

A soft footstep drew Dave's heightened attention and he felt a familiar hand caress his hair. He leaned into his mother's touch.

"Come, my child," soothed Nightingale's soft voice. "The night is late, and we have much to do."

Relic

It was a moment of true wonder.

The sturdy chains creaked and the peering onlookers held their breath as the swaying crane tentatively eased the last remaining chunk of ancient detritus out of the archaeological pit. The patchwork of old stone and rubble wobbled like an uncertain octogenarian as it rose hesitantly into the expectant air before being gently lowered to the awaiting space at the side of the dig.

The site supervisor barged his way to the front of the rubbernecking crowd. He was normally a quiet man, content to just chip away at the layers of accumulated dust and dirt that had covered civilisation over the millennia of time, but today he was having to raise his voice to be heard. "Back! Back, I say! Everyone back! Let me through."

A reporter tried to push a camera into the squat, little man's face. The supervisor grabbed it by the lens and shoved hard causing the intruder to swear loudly. He had no time for any of these frivolities. He had work to do. This was the greatest find of the century and it needed cataloguing, preserving and studying. His breath came in short, hard gasps and his skin sweated profusely as he finally managed to elbow his way to the edge of the pit. "Well?" he shouted down.

About five metres down, two members of his team were busily brushing away dust and fragments of earth from the now exposed surface.

"Well?" the supervisor enquired again, his voice squeaking with agitated falsetto. "What's down there?"

One of the archaeologists looked up, beaming from under his protective hat. "It's amazing, Sir. Truly amazing."

And it was.

It took another month to extract the relic from the archaeological pit and what a month it was. The media hype had shot around the world like flame on gunpowder. All manner of theories had started to spring up as to what the item actually was: some thoughtful, some absurd. Such was the nature of humanity, the supervisor pondered as he regarded the thing of ancient beauty that lay in front of him under the temporary canvas roof of the site's mobile headquarters.

Tenderly, he ran a callused finger along the rough edge of the artefact, smiling wistfully as he did so. It had been quite a struggle to extricate it from the pit. The relic had quite obviously been part of a larger construction at one point – there were jagged edges to some of the curious round stones that made up its main body – but something had caused it to fracture. Perhaps subsidence or geological pressures over the years had snapped the item into smaller pieces? The man shook his head at the wonder that there might be more of this curious object down under the earth: still buried, awaiting discovery.

His eyes travelled between the round, interlocking lattice of stone that rose and fell like a vast range of hills, a rolling countryside. Although the stones were similar in size and dimension – approximately ten centimetres across – they were by no means uniform. Some were slightly larger, some smaller. Was there a meaning to this? Was there a pattern here that he had yet to decipher? His trembling hand ran tremulously over his balding scalp. There were also small gaps between the stones as if there had been something there in times gone past that was now missing. He had theorised that organic matter had once dwelt there but had rotted away over the years. His team were still scouring every nook and cranny for evidence of wood, grass, seeds or any other material to verify this. It was indeed a painstaking job.

Then there was the script.

There was not much of it, but it was clear and evident for all to see. This was what had caused the excitement on the day of the excavation. It was brilliant white and scrolled its way across five of the stones.

It was causing a headache extraordinaire.

There was no record of this writing form in any of the extensive databases through which the supervisor and his team had searched. They had rooted through archive after archive trying to match this scrolling penmanship but there was nothing at all that was even a close match. It had them completely confounded. This was, to say the least, problematic. The powers that be had invested a huge amount of finance into this excavation and they demanded results. They were sending specialists over this afternoon to examine the script. Apparently, political pressure was being applied to the backers of the project and with times being what they were that meant someone's head could roll.

Or worse.

The supervisor regarded his timepiece. It was almost time for the so-called specialists to arrive. Would they be able to decipher the code or would they be just as stumped as he was? He was guessing the latter and that worried him greatly.

"As we can see from the way that this character here quite clearly links the two on either side, we can be sure that this is a call to the faithful visiting the shrine."

Heads bobbed up and down, intent on demonstrating sage wisdom when the brains contained within did not have the foggiest idea as to what the speaker was explaining.

The relic had been a resident at the Chatterton Institute for around five months now and had been subjected to every possible form of analysis that a league of esteemed academics could apply. The result was this weeklong symposium where the greatest minds hid their bafflement at what was still a total enigma. True, some of fine academics got up and made very colourful descriptions about what they believed the artefact to be, but their surrounding peers knew better. It was all gibberish. The scientific community was at a complete dead end.

Other groups, though, had different ideas. There had been rumours circulating that idealistic factions wanted to take control of the artefact. They claimed that the scientists were, in fact, hiding something dark and insidious. Theories and speculative ideas had now started to surface from the more radical quarters of society. As a result, security at the symposium was tantamount.

However, one cannot inhibit a driven radical from his or her purpose.

Rapid gunfire rattled through the hall and terrified scientists dove for cover as some guards fell to the floor dead whilst others unshouldered their arms and returned defensive fire. Canisters flew into the vast room and smoke started to snake its way out of the small cylinders. The guards and the scientists coughed and gagged as they gasped for air until in a few seconds they lay still and immobile.

Masked figures stalked their way through the smoke, wary in case anyone was playing possum. Their guns flicked left and right, nervously. When they were sure that they were the only living souls in the room, a giant of a man strode up to the artefact, regarded it from behind his mask as a one might look upon a beautiful predator, unsure whether to be in awe of its sleek design or terrified that it might snap its jaws around one's middle. Eventually he nodded slowly and smiled behind his faceplate. He signalled for his men to come forward with chains and a gurney.

The relic belonged to them now. With it they would build a new tomorrow.

"Today sees the birth of a new world!"

The video footage was grainy, amateur. The camera shook as if it was not attached to a tripod but was instead held tightly by an overexcited disciple of the cause.

"We, and only we," continued the speaker, a tall man dressed head to toe in white, "know the truth to the mystical writing that was unearthed and stolen from public view by the Chatterton Institute. This," the camera zoomed in hastily on the artefact at which the speaker was pointing, "is a legacy from our past. It was inscribed by wise men who knew that we held our lives in our hands. It tells of days to come when the oppressed shall rise up and claim what is rightfully theirs. It was written..."

He never finished his sentence.

A shot rang out and a red dot appeared on his forehead as a look of disbelief took control of his facial muscles before he fell backwards to the floor.

The camera swung round to capture a squad of black clad soldiers bursting into view. One raised his gun to the lens and then there was static.

"This cannot be permitted to continue."

The voice was calm and clipped but unbridled anger bubbled under the surface.

"No, Sir."

"We must claim the Chatterton Stones for ourselves, for our people."

"Yes, Sir."

From his luxurious seat behind his mammoth mahogany desk, the ruler of the most powerful country on the planet peered over steepled finger-tips at his entourage of advisers. Advisers? They were anything but. They were just a bunch of fawning Yes Men: bringing him Cappuccinos, sorting his mail and agreeing with whatever he said. If he told them to go jump in the lake outside his office then they would do so gladly with beatific smiles on their faces.

And that was exactly what he wanted.

There was no room for advice nowadays. What was needed was vision and action; and right now he was going to act. "Is the task force ready?"

"Yes, Sir."

He nodded. "Then send them in."

"It's no good, Sir. They have broken into the compound."

Another leader from another country looked out over another entourage of Yes Men. "The Chatterton Stones?"

The advisers looked cautiously from one to another. Terror bounced back and forth between their eyes as they mentally drew straws. Eventually, one poor soul lost. "They have been extracted by the hostiles." He cringed awaiting the wrath of his leader.

Instead, there was a pondering silence.

After what seemed like an hour but was in reality just a few seconds, the same adviser asked, "Sir, what do you want to do?"

The leader sat back in his swivel chair and stared out of the window. From this high up he could see most of the capital. Down there, men and women went to work, children played and innocents carried on with their everyday lives.

Lives that would be ruined if his country's enemies cracked the code that was scrawled across the Chatterton Stones.

He could not let that happen.

"Order a pre-emptive strike," he whispered, "and may God have mercy on our souls."

Before the first missile struck, a reciprocating flotilla of devastation had been launched in the opposite direction. The fire of jet propulsion burned up into the fragile atmosphere and guided the rockets to their doomed targets. All hit with deadly precision. The Earth's atmosphere was set aglow with the impacts. Mushroom clouds billowed up to the stratosphere, scorching the ground, poisoning the air and slaughtering millions in a matter of minutes.

There were inevitable repercussions. For too long the world had been teetering on the brink of oblivion. For millennia, the planet's inhabitants had borne the interminable load packed to the brim with grudges of hate and spite whilst sharpening their blades in silence. These acts of aggression from the highest levels unstopped the dams that had held back the flow of pent up hatred and homicide. Country turned on country, neighbour turned on neighbour, child turned on parent. Within a matter of days the entire planet was consuming itself in an orgy of bilious devastation. The population declined within weeks as its inhabitants bled to death in the deserted streets and the leaders of humanity were now impotent, unable to prevent the onslaught or turn back the raging waters of the dam that had been breached.

No one tended the fields.

No one fed the livestock.

Energy supplies became erratic and the sick were left to die.

Within a year the human race was a mere shadow of its former glory. It slunk off, found itself a dark hole in which to hide and there, pondering how all this could have come about over a collection of old stones covered in unintelligible writing, it curled up, closed its eyes and breathed its last.

"Damn it!"

Colin Gibson eased himself up from the kneeling position in front of his white Ford Cortina. He had completed the touch up job underneath the bumper where the rust had been speckling through the paintwork, but he had managed to drip some of the white paint on the cobbles between the weeds that always seemed to poke their way up no matter what he threw at them.

He shook his head. He really should have used spray paint rather than the old tin of gloss he had found kicking around under the sink. The gloss covered the rust great but it was a pain to clean up.

He shrugged as he snapped the lid back on the tin.

Ah well. A bit of paint on some old cobbles was

24

hardly a disaster was it?

Test Flight

Goldblum grappled with the joystick as the plane jinked and jerked from side to side. The webbing dug in tight whilst his eyes widened at the sight of the cliff face looming rapidly like a ravening giant.

At the last moment, his hands flew from the controls to instinctively cover his face from the inevitable collision.

Saunders tutted sympathetically as his associate pulled yet another lifeless body out of the X-20 simulator. Feeling the lack of pulse on the latest test pilot, he turned and asked of his fellow technician, "Do you think we've made this thing rather too realistic?"

Second Time Around

The bar stank of warm beer, hormonal sweat and stale urine. These were not aromas that pleased the smartly dressed woman who resided in a corner booth whilst she nursed a poorly made cocktail. Her preferences lingered more in the exotic: drifting incense, burning coals and sweet perfumes. The fragrances of devotion, not boredom.

A smile touched her perfectly glossed lips as she remembered better times and she played idly with the artificially coloured red cherry which was impaled on a cheap cocktail stick. A droplet of her feeble excuse for a drink rolled down the fruit's surface and dripped towards the table. The woman frowned and the alcohol hovered in mid-air, never reaching the sticky woodwork. Slowly, it defied all laws of gravity and rose upwards before starting to spin ferociously, gaining momentum. The woman stared intently at the droplet, watching the dim lights of the student bar flicker in its surface before pointing a slender, manicured finger at the liquid and sending it hurtling across the room.

A young male clasped his hand to the back of his neck and turned round, glowering with anger as he tried to spot who had just flicked something at him. His eyes found the woman and she smiled at him, knowingly.

He smiled back.

She drained her drink, rose gracefully from her seat and walked past the young man as she exited the bar. He trailed obediently behind. The woman smiled as she scented a new aroma on the air.

Desire.

Slowly, she walked her way down the covered pathway of the urban campus, her red heels clicking enticingly on the paving slabs as they encouraged the young man to keep up. As she turned a corner she paused and watched him staggering hungrily behind her. She needed no beckoning gesture, no come-hither. He was her's, utterly and completely.

The alley down which she walked darkened as the overhead lighting became more infrequent. This was a forgotten area where staff and students rarely ventured; a dead spot on the campus. The woman arrived at a place where a rusting door hung askance from its frame. Not wanting to damage her perfect nails, the woman extended her hand and a thin stream of water extruded from her fingertips. It pressed against the old door and forced it open, allowing her unhindered access.

The young man followed her into the dark storeroom. "I'm yours," he whispered hoarsely.

"I know," came a deeply sensual voice in reply. "You always have been. You always will be." Her manicured fingers ran up his chest and around his neck, drawing him close. The man gasped as she latched his mouth onto hers.

He kissed her wildly.

She let him.

His hands ran over her back and through her hair.

She thought about legions of worshippers bowing down before her under an excruciatingly hot sun.

His fingers ran up her front and found her soft breast.

She remembered the smell of blood and entrails spewing from those sacrificed solely for her amusement.

He started to gag and splutter. The woman's fingers gripped his head tight and locked his mouth against hers. Water trickled slowly from the seal of their lips.

The man's eyes flashed in terror and the last thing he saw was a pair of flames peering curiously at him.

Then there was blackness.

"Having fun?"

Asherah ignored the mocking male voice as she let her lip-gloss adjust itself whilst she stepped out of the storeroom.

"So what? You're just going to leave it there?"

Her locks of hair tidied themselves as she stopped, sighed and said, "You were late. I was bored."

There was the sound of footsteps and her interrogator stepped into view, the feeble light casting an unhealthy sheen to his sallow skin. "One of these days you'll get caught, and what will you do then?"

"Like you really care for my well-being. You're just concerned that I'll drag you down with me." She turned and carried on walking. He fell in step at her side. "So why were you late, as if I really care?"

"I've been shopping."

She eyed him up and down from the corner of her eye. His long, black coat almost touched the floor as he walked. "Can't see any difference. You still look like a reject from an Anne Rice novel."

Her companion reached into his coat, ignoring the insult. "Got myself this."

Asherah sighed again as she glanced briefly at the gleaming, brand new pistol. "What on Earth do you need that for? You can just bore people to death."

"I liked the look of it," he explained, pointing the gun at random pieces of stonework and glancing down the sight. "It goes with the image."

"Really, Asmodeus! Tell me for the umpteenth time, why did we leave Heaven?"

"Don't start on about that again."

"You're just one bright idea after another, aren't you?"

"It wasn't my fault! It was..."

Asherah flapped an annoyed hand at her fellow angel. "Don't say it! Don't mention his name. Don't ever mention his name. Remember the last time we crossed his path?"

Asmodeus nodded as he stowed the gun away. "Too well."

They walked on in contemplative silence until the female angel finally said, "I'm going to be uncontactable for a while. That's why I needed to see you."

"Oh? I thought you had a thing going on here? With that student."

"Malcolm?" Asherah nodded. "I did, but he's getting so intense. It's all when are we going to destroy the world? I've had enough. I'm going to ditch him tonight and head off on my own for a bit."

They were now walking back up to the main square of the campus. The bars had emptied and they were alone, all except for a lone figure sat on the steps at the far side of the square.

"That him?"

Asherah nodded.

"Good luck," Asmodeus said and slipped away leaving her on her own.

The former goddess of Canaan gave herself a quick mental check over and walked across the square to her last remaining disciple.

A puppy dog. A small, bouncy terrier that's so eager to please, Asherah thought as she climbed the staircase, her young disciple, Malcolm Wallace chattering away excitedly in front of her. "So, let me get this straight," she said out loud as they emerged onto the youth's corridor, "you persuaded your friends to recite an incantation which would bind a ghost to the physical realm?"

Wallace nodded, his strange orange pupils bouncing up and down with delight. "Sam fell for it completely."

"How?"

31

"He's desperate to know what's going to happen to his terminally ill father when he dies."

Asherah paused and ran a polished nail against Wallace's cheek. "That's terribly wicked. I like it." She thought Wallace was going to faint with joy right there. She would give him five minutes, see what he had to show her then kill him before heading off into the night with whatever she felt like from his personal stash of paraphernalia.

"Are they in there?" She nodded over Wallace's shoulder to the glass door leading into what appeared to be a kitchen. She could make out two figures slumped over a table.

Wallace nodded again, turned, looked in the kitchen then his face fell. Asherah immediately realised what was wrong. His friends were alone.

"No ghosty," she whispered and pushed past into the room, her heels clicking on the tiled floor. Slowly, she glanced around, not just with her eyes but with all her senses and intuition. The two fellow students seemed to be fast asleep, there was the unmistakable smell of beer in the air and there was an empty chair at the head of the table. As Asherah glided past the chair and let her fingers run along its back, she felt an unmistakable tingle shimmy up her spine causing her to smile. There had been something else here; something supernatural. Perhaps it had escaped or perhaps...

Perhaps these two youths had managed to rid themselves of it.

She looked from one to the other. One was slightly overweight, sporting a downy boy-beard and roaring louder than a bad-tempered dromedary. The other was of average height with a mop of curly hair and...

Asherah had to prevent herself from taking a sharp intake of breath. Hello, she thought. What have we here? Her heels continued to click purposefully as she circled the table and reached the curly-haired youth. There was something about him, something she could not quite pin down.

It intrigued her.

That certainly beat being bored.

She let her nails stroke up the boy's neck and into his hair causing him to groan slightly in his sleep. "This one's rather cute," she said over her shoulder as Wallace entered the room, a thundercloud rumbling above his head.

"They must have removed him before we got here," he grumbled as he wrote something down on a scrap of paper. "Shame. I would have liked to see the looks on their faces."

Asherah's manicured nails continued to play with the curly hair as she decided that she would like to see the look on the youth's face too. She started to hum a low tune under her breath. The boy gasped sharply in his slumber and she felt his body tense with arousal.

"Stop that!" Wallace hissed. "We don't have time."

Asherah ceased her little tune and the boy settled back down to sleep. There was not enough time now, but there would be in the future, she decided. Perhaps Wallace could be of use to her after all? He could suit her needs and then, when his path crossed with this youth's again, she would jump ship and let her student sink ignominiously into the Abyss.

"Later," she whispered to the sleeping boy before stalking out of the room. Wallace shoved the piece of paper into his friend's hand and followed her down the stairwell. "Tell me Malcolm," the goddess purred, "have I ever told you about The Divergence?" She turned to face her disciple and...

...stood outside watching Asmodeus slinking off into the shadows. "Good luck," he called over his shoulder.

Asherah spun on her heels, suddenly dizzy and confused. This was not right. This had already happened.

Along with a shed load of other things.

She remembered them happening.

With her long-time partner in crime gone, she turned and looked out once more into the square. Wallace was there again, but this time he was not alone. When the angel saw who was with him, she could not help but smile. "Well, hello," she grinned. "Fancy meeting you here," she murmured under her breath.

It was the curly-haired boy from the kitchen, but he had grown up and Asherah liked how he had grown. He oozed anger and hatred and...

"Apparently he can fly," she mused to herself as the man grabbed Wallace by the neck then jumped up to the top of the old chimney that adorned the corner of the square. Leaning against a pillar, Asherah beamed at the sound of her disciple screaming pitifully in the night. "Aww, widdle baby," she laughed, raising her hand to her mouth to stifle her chuckles. This was hilarious. She had not had so much fun since... Well, for a very long time, at least. Who was this stranger? He was intoxicating. He stood at the top of the chimney holding onto a writhing Wallace. "Let go, let go, let go," Asherah hissed, pounding a fist into her hand. "I want to see him fall."

She was not disappointed.

"Oh, that's gotta hurt," she jeered as her disciple smacked into the hard paving slabs. However, it was not over yet. The stranger jumped easily from the chimney top and glided down to the body of his victim. He stood there, looking down at Wallace drumming his fingers on his teeth before crouching down as if something was wrong.

Asherah gave a start when she saw the apparently dead Wallace's hand shoot up and grab his assailant by the wrist. "Now, who's been doing extra homework?" she purred, her eyes bright with fire and glee. The two males went at it tooth and claw, pounding with fists and slapping with words until finally the stranger appeared to have to upper hand. Then, for the second time that night, Asherah felt truly amazed as she heard three non-words leave the stranger's mouth.

"..."

"..."

"..."

"How?" she gasped, truly shocked. "That's not possible. How could he?" The portal to Beyond flared open as she tried to work out how the stranger had learnt the incantation that Asmodeus had taught her and she had passed on to Wallace. They were the only three creatures in existence who knew how to do that.

Until now, apparently.

This was marvellous! She strode across the square, clapping slowly as she did. "Oh, well done. Well done indeed," she offered in congratulation as the victor looked over. A glimmer of recognition seemed to light his face as he glanced down at his prey then back up to her. She wandered idly over to some stone steps and settled herself down, stretching her legs out in front of her. "Well, go on then."

"Pardon?" The man's voice cracked as he spoke and a slight air of confusion swept across his face.

She pointed to the portal with a finely manicured finger. "Finish him off. I don't have all night and I've been so looking forward to this." Smiling her cruellest smile, she gave full reassurance that she was deadly serious.

The man's concentration had obviously been broken as Wallace rolled out from underneath him. "What do you mean?" her disciple whined. "You can't be serious!"

Asherah sighed. Here we go, she thought. Mister Petulant. She made as if she were studying her nails and changed the hue of their varnish a few times before looking up and saying, "Oh, are you still here? Not taken over the world yet? You know that gets so dull in the end. 'Look, look, here's the universe I destroyed for you!' Bor-ring." She turned her attention to the stranger. "I've had an eternity of that you know. It's okay the first few times, but its gets dull ever so quickly." The thing was, she realised, that she wholeheartedly meant it. Here she was, a fallen angel, doomed to walk amongst lesser beings who would become infatuated with her and promise her the world and its apocalypse over and over again. It was just so monotonous.

This guy, however...

Asherah smiled. He felt different. As he stood there breathing heavily, his eyes darting from her to Wallace then to the portal, he presented no signs that he needed to fall down and worship her, no desire to be a mindless minion.

He felt unique.

Unlike Wallace who was now snivelling and begging her to let him live. "You can't do this," he whined. "We had plans."

"You had plans!" Asherah had had enough and she snapped at him like a serpent at a rodent. "I was just having fun and now I'm not. You're boring, Malcolm. So damned boring." She stood in one fluid move. "I'm through with you. Finished."

"Please, please don't leave me." Good grief he was actually weeping now. Pitiful. "What will I do without you?"

Asherah looked up at the ball of hatred that stood behind her former disciple and, for a brief moment, she was no longer standing in a paved square of a small town university. She saw the insides of a small cellar where an older version of Wallace stood gloating before sending an unfortunate teenage boy through the same portal that stood dangerously next to him in the here and now. Asherah nodded in realisation of what she had seen through the stranger's eyes. "Quite frankly, after what you are going to do to his son, I really don't think that's an issue. Goodbye, Malcolm."

With that, she turned and walked away, hiding the beaming grin on her face. Life was going to be so much more fun the second time around.

Needs Must

It was a nice well: roomy, dank and dark. There was just a glimmer of hurtful sunlight from the small aperture high above. This suited Odd Bod, suited him fine. As he sat in the noxious gloop that constituted the well's floor he scratched the infrequent tufts of hair on his scabrous scalp and decided that, overall, life had been very good to him. He had a safe place to live and there had been no hordes of angry villagers chasing him with pitchforks or other horticultural accoutrements.

The food, however, was becoming a problem.

Odd Bod tugged at a small bone that was lodged in the sticky floor and it parted company from the clinging substance with a wet pop. He blew at it and a piece of green slime dripped onto his knee. Absentmindedly rubbing at the slime with one hand, his other used the bone as an impromptu toothpick between his blackened incisors whilst he contemplated the issue of supplies.

There used to be plenty of food. It would come to the well, drop the wooden thing down to scoop up

39

the wet stuff and, if he was hungry, Odd Bod would give the wooden thing a big tug causing the food to come crashing down into his awaiting lap. True, it was a noisy experience when the food fell and sometimes it needed convincing that it really was food but on the whole it worked to Odd Bod's satis-faction.

Recently though the food had stopped dropping the wooden thing down. Odd Bod thought that this must be down to one of two reasons. It was either because the horrid wet stuff that the wooden thing used to scoop up had finally vanished or, and this possibility troubled Odd Bod more, that he had eaten all the food and there was none left.

Yes, that troubled Odd Bod a great deal. The thought of a world with no food was not a pleasant prospect at all even if he did live in a very nice dark, dank well with very little sunlight.

He hoped that it was the lack of the wet stuff that had caused the food to go away, he truly did because if the wet stuff came back then the food would, too. If, however, he had eaten all the food...

Odd Bod sadly shook his head. He had never been a fan of the wet stuff. It had always gotten everywhere and had made him feel as icky as the wet stuff itself. Odd Bod had fashioned himself small ledges between the crumbling bricks which had provided places for him to perch on when the wet stuff had risen up at certain times of the year. Then over the last few years the wet stuff had stopped rising. Instead, it had gotten lower and lower until all that was left was the gloop and the bits of broken bone that Odd Bod had discarded during his time in the well.

Odd Bod liked the gloop. It stuck nicely to his bony fingers and made his nose wrinkle when he sniffed it. Much more pleasant than the wet stuff.

However, if the wet stuff going away had caused his food to disappear then that was a bad thing, whether Odd Bod liked the wet stuff or not, and something had to be done about it. The melancholy creature looked up to the small hole high above and sighed. There was only one way to find out what had happened to his food. Had it gone away or had it all been eaten? He had to find out or he would starve. It would not be the easiest of jobs, but one that had to be undertaken, nonetheless. His stomach rumbled and he whimpered disconsolately, his shaggy whiskers quivering around his mouth.

Odd Bod transferred the small bone from his hand to between his freshly picked teeth and placed a bare foot onto the lowest of the perches. He reached up with his hands - his cracked and broken nails searching out the tiniest of nooks and crannies with which to heave himself up. A foot edged up to another perch and his hands started to seek out more holes where he could cling securely between the bricks. After he had reached the same number of perches as he had fingers on his left hand he had to start work with the bone. Whilst clinging on with one set of fingers, the others used the bone to dig out handholds and footholds for him to utilise.

So it went on, time after time, transferring his weight onto newly excavated holes whilst digging out more and more spaces for his hands and feet. As he ascended the side of the well Odd Bod realised that the work was becoming harder and harder. Down below, the wall had been soft and easier to excavate. Up higher, it was tough and the bricks were much more firmly cemented together, but Odd Bod knew there could be no turning back. He peered down between his legs at his comfortable home and whimpered plaintively. What he would give to be settled down there once more with some fresh food, happily enjoying the knobbly, gristly bits that spurted goo all down his front as his teeth chomped into them. Instead, his muscles ached and his throat was dry. Moreover, to make matters worse, he was starting to feel very warm.

Odd Bod looked up and saw the reason for the increased heat: the hole at the top of the well was getting much larger! He had thought it was starting to increase in width when he had reached about half way but he had dismissed the notion as silliness. Now, however, here he was, much higher up and the round hole was definitely letting in more of the hated sunlight. Odd Bod blinked as the brightness hurt his eyes and he focussed yet again on the task at hand, digging furiously between two stubborn bricks. Even the bricks seemed to be suffering from the sunshine. Down below, they had been beautifully dark and shiny; up here, they were dry and much paler in colour. Odd Bod shuddered as he dreaded what the evil sunshine would do to him when he eventually emerged from the well.

He carried on climbing.

In time, his breathing became somewhat laboured as his throat felt parched. Odd Bod started to whimper as he began to fear that he was not going to make it to the top of the well. Despair started to wash over him.

What if he slipped and fell? Would he make the same noises that the food normally made when it jumped down to him?

What if he got to the top and discovered that he had eaten all the food? His stomach roared and he shook his head. No, he must not think such things. Food had to be out there. It had just gone away when the wet stuff had disappeared!

He glanced up and squeaked in both fear and excitement. Fear because the hole was now so wide that he could not see all the way around it. Excitement because he was only about an arm's length from the top. A broad grin of blackened teeth spread across his face and he clambered towards the rim of the well.

Odd Bod's stomach lurched as his foot slipped and his arm swung free. Screaming loudly he gripped with one hand on the bone that was currently dug between two bricks.

Silly Odd Bod!
Silly Odd Bod!

He had let his excitement get the better of him and had lost his concentration. With one firm tug on the bone, he swung his loose arm up and grabbed at the tiniest of gaps in the unforgiving brickwork. His nails prised themselves in and he hissed in pain as the rough surface dug into his grey flesh. Desperately, his feet scrambled at the sheer wall below him, propelling his weight up towards the rim of the well. He discarded the bone, ignoring the tool as it tumbled down towards the dark, comforting gloop.

Instead, he hauled his hand up to the precipice above him. His fingers flailed around crumbling material on the rim until they found sound purchase and the rest of his withered body scurried up the last little distance. With one, firm lunge he heaved himself up and over the edge of the well. He rolled head over heels and landed with a thump on something that was most definitely not gloop.

Odd Bod bent over onto all fours and peered closely at the stuff. It covered the floor around the well. It felt strange to his gloop-accustomed touch and consisted of a multitude of little strands of near identical material that stood together in the near vicinity.

He sniffed it. It wobbled as he did so.

Carefully he picked some out and stuck it in his mouth before chewing.

"Pah!" He spat the disgusting substance out and wiped spittle from his face with the back of his dirt-encrusted hand.

"Why are you eating grass?"

Odd Bod's head snapped up and his eyes located the source of the noise. It was food; a small morsel, but food nonetheless. He grinned.

The food giggled as it clasped its hands over its mouth. "You look funny," it laughed.

Odd Bod sat down on the horrid-tasting stuff and scratched his threadbare scalp. This food was strange. Food normally made noises like, "Oh, God! No! No!" or "Please no! I have children!" This one sounded different. In addition, it was not covered in delicious icky stuff.

He pointed with a chipped and broken fingernail. "Food?" his gravelly voice enquired.

"Sure," said the little red-haired girl. "I've got lots. Teddy and I are having a tea party on the blanket over there."

Odd Bod's eyes followed her small finger as it pointed over to a small furry thing sat on the thing called a blanket. "Food?" he asked again.

The little girl walked over to him and took his warty hand in hers. "Come on. We have plenty."

Odd Bod clambered to his feet and slowly lurched along behind her as she led him over to the blanket where the small, inanimate furry thing was propped up against a grey stone. In front of it were a number of round receptacles of different sizes along with an object that had a handle on one side and a pointy bit on the other. The girl patted the blanket next to her and Odd Bod seated himself down, tucking his gangly legs beneath him. He frowned as his brain used to years of peaceful solitude tried to make sense of the situation. As his grey cells bumped together in confusion, the little girl handed him one of the round things. "Here you go," she said. "Cake."

The very perplexed diner took the object in both his hands and stared at it. It was flat and about the size of one of his hands. It was decorated around the edge with pink flowers. Not sure what to do, he shoved it in his mouth and started to chew.

"No!" exclaimed the girl, leaning over and dragging the thing out of his mouth. "Don't eat the plate. Eat the cake." She proceeded to hold her own plate and apparently feasted on thin air.

Odd Bod did likewise. The air did not taste of

anything. He frowned.

"It is only make-believe, you know," the girl whispered into his ear. "There isn't really any cake. Just don't tell Teddy. He'll get upset."

Odd Bod looked over at Teddy. The small, furry thing was making no apparent effort to eat the make-believe cake. Whatever cake was. Odd Bod sighed and glanced longingly over his shoulder to his well.

"Are you thirsty?"

"Thirsty?" Odd Bod asked.

The girl was now placing a different receptacle in front of him. This one was also decorated in flowers but was somewhat deeper in shape. "I'll pour some nice tea in the cups." She picked up the odd-looking thing with the handle and poured a clear liquid into the cups before offering one to her guest. "Here you go."

Odd Bod took the little cup awkwardly in his misshapen fingers and raised it to his mouth. His nose caught a whiff of its smell and wrinkled in disgust. He snapped his head back and grimaced.

"Now, don't be rude," the little redhead scowled. "Drink it all up."

Odd Bod looked across the rim of the cup to this strange piece of food that was not acting as it should then peered down into the cup unsure as to what he should do. Part of him wanted to reach over and gobble her up but part of him felt he really ought to do as he was told. It was only polite.

He placed the cup to his lips.

The girl smiled and nodded for him to continue. "Down in one," she said.

Odd Bod did as he was instructed and gulped the liquid down.

He immediately regretted the decision.

Emily carefully tidied up the blanket and the tea set. She cautiously poured the remains of the so-called tea down the dry, foul-smelling well - the well in which her mummy had died. She had no idea what she had put in the teapot but it seemed to have done the trick. It had been a concoction of all sorts of liquids from tins in the cellar, the labels of which had borne loud warning symbols.

It had worked a treat.

She had been terribly scared when the monster had climbed out of the well, but it had saved her the job of climbing down to do what had needed doing. Besides, Teddy had been there for moral support.

The thing that had eaten her mummy and so many other villagers lay dead at her feet.

She bundled Teddy and the tea set into the blanket, swung the improvised bag over her shoulder and skipped merrily home.

Just Like Everybody Else

So, have you ever wanted to kill someone?

Now, I don't mean that silly little thing where you get mad at some idiot who cuts you up on the motorway and you shout out, "Oh, I could kill you, darn it!" No, not that. Nor when your loved one has let you down at the last minute for some romantic soirée or some such and you say, "Wait till I get my hands on him..." and so on, and so on.

No, I don't mean that at all.

That's not really wanting to kill someone, is it? That's just getting a bit ticked off when you feel rather annoyed. You crease your brow, thump your fists onto your hips and just vent whatever comes into your mouth. There might be some choice language, some expletives, other such stuff and then you say that you want to kill someone.

You don't really want to kill them. You want to punish them but right there and then you are so miffed that you can't think of the appropriate retribution to inflict so you just say that you want to kill them.

48

That's not what I mean at all.

I mean, have you ever really wanted to kill someone? Have you wanted to extinguish their light, snuff out their candle or obliterate any other such twee cliché that we use when we say that someone has been removed from mortal existence.

That sort of kill someone.

Of course you have.

We all have.

Don't deny it. I can tell. You're blushing, so it must be true. You're sitting there, reading this and shifting uncomfortably in your seat. Perhaps you're on the bus, riding to work next to that guy who never bathes or you're curled up in bed with your loved one as they softly snore themselves to sleep? You could be anywhere, but right now you're thinking to yourself: How does he know?

Well, the answer to that is simple.

We all want to do it at some point in our life. After all, it's only human.

We all have urges.

Sure, there are the urges that we will happily talk about to friends and family: we get hungry, we get tired, we feel horny. These are all socially acceptable to a certain degree, but that same society frowns so deeply on the one urge that constantly niggles away at the back of our head.

The need to kill.

I wonder why that is?

If it's there, it must be perfectly natural, surely? If it wasn't then evolution would have stripped it from us the moment we jumped down from the trees and started wandering around on two feet. Perhaps it's some archaic psychological trauma, founded from when we were prey and watched our loved ones being feasted upon by those wild monsters further up the primal food chain? Perhaps it's our need for dominance over those around us to ensure that our seed continues to thrive?

Perhaps.

I'm not convinced though.

I'm more inclined to think it's our brain doing a bit of judicial weeding of society. Let's face it, we all have our own ideas as to what is right and what is wrong. Surely we want to see those personal norms spread through our community and the wider world? What's a more effective way of making sure that those values survive than removing those individuals that oppose them? We see it all the time at the international level. Governments sanction the deaths of those who stand against them either through war, assassination or execution, so what's to stop us doing it at a somewhat lower level?

You, on the bus: the guy next to you who always smells and hasn't seen a bath for an eternity - he repulses you, doesn't he? Follow him one day and get rid of him. One less smelly guy.

You, with the snoring partner. What do you think pillows were really invented for?

Try it.

It's liberating.

Anyway, I'm rambling here. Where was I?

Oh, yes. Urges.

We all have them, but what's the best way to follow them through?

"Well, I could get myself a gun and blow

someone's head off," I hear you cry. Really? You think it's that simple? Sure, if you want to get caught! Don't you ever watch CSI? Police are quite clever these days; they use science. Everyone knows that each gun has its own fingerprint. The bullet leaves the barrel at a certain speed or angle and can be quickly matched to a specific gun. No, if you use a gun then your killing will have been in vain. They'll catch you, lock you up and throw away the key.

And don't get me started on strangling. Go ahead, compress someone's carotid artery and see how far that gets you. There's bound to be finger-prints, some trace of fabric or your DNA under the victim's fingernails as they fight frantically for their life. No, you strangle someone you might as well walk into a police station with a large cardboard sign around your neck saying, "I did it!"

Poison? So you're a trained chemist now, are you? Jesus! Have you looked at all those potential victims around you? Are they all the same size? Do they all have the same metabolism? Not a chance; far too risky. You could slip them a Mickey, sit back and watch them just get incredibly giggly. Now wouldn't that be annoying? Worse still, you might achieve a less than half-decent job and they could come staggering at you across the room gagging and frothing at the mouth as they try to rip your eyes out. Not a pretty sight, I'm telling you.

No. There is only one, sure-fire way to kill someone.

A knife.

Small, sharp and thrust quickly in the side. Make sure you hit a major organ or rummage around so much that they bleed out rapidly. Okay, it's messy. Not a method you'd want to do on your favourite Persian rug, I agree, but it's effective.

It's also satisfying, the feeling of their life gently ebbing away as you cradle them in your arms.

Blissful.

For the ones you like, that is.

The ones you hate? Just slit their wretched necks and be done with it. Probably best standing on a bridge at the time so you can push them into the water and watch them drown bloodily. Very gratifying.

Ah, the very thought of it; taking someone who you want removed and dispatching them quickly and efficiently.

Yes! There you go. That little glint in your eye and the quick intake of breath. You saw it, didn't you? Just for a second. You saw the look on their face when you plunged the blade in: the shock, the confusion. You felt the rush of satisfaction: the total, utter glee. It won't leave you now. It's there, imprinted on your retinas. Perhaps they throw their head back slightly in pain as you witness a stretched artery pumping futilely while their blood gushes from their wound onto the floor? Yes, perhaps.

You're licking your lips and you don't know why. You're not hungry for food, but you crave something else.

Something deeper.

Something insatiable.

Now you know what I mean. Now you hear what I'm saying.

You're just like everybody else. You're just like

me and I'm just like you. The question is, "What are you going to do about it?"

I know what I'm going to do. The only question is, to whom?

Perhaps it might be you?

Prodigy

"Well, obviously we are so very pleased with Charlie's progress."

A perfectly chilled bottle of Chardonnay was tilted and crisply fragranced wine poured into an expensive crystal glass. Harrison smiled and raised the receptacle to his lips before sipping slowly. He had to admit it was a very fine flavour and made the prolonged torture of his hosts' waffling somewhat more bearable. "So what can he do these days?" He volunteered the question in the pretence that he was genuinely interested. In truth he would much rather have been out on the golf course enjoying the sun on his face and the adoring looks of the rather cute caddy that had recently started carrying his clubs.

"Oh, all sorts of things!" Charlie's mother chipped in brightly.

Harrison groaned inwardly. That was all he needed; the blonde vacuum had been switched on. How Clarke could live with such a ditz was completely beyond him. He may be interminably dull but had an incredibly incisive brain. Perhaps it was just the sex? Anyway, now she had started to whitter on there would be no stopping her. He took a larger sip of the finely fragranced wine and braced himself.

"There's all that clever stuff with the letters, isn't there Ronnie?"

"Algebra, Dear."

"Yes, that's right. Algebra," she giggled, scooping a few pretzels out of a lacquered fair trade bowl from Borneo. "I mean, who would have thought? Sums using letters! What will be next? Stories written in numbers?"

Her childish giggle seared into Harrison's brain like a stun gun into an unlucky future pork chop. He surreptitiously glanced at his watch. Christ! It was only three! He took a mental breath. "Algebra? Really? Fascinating. How old is the little man, now?"

"He's not five until September," Clarke said. "He'll be one of the oldest children in his year group. I guess that will give him a bit of an advantage."

"Five?" Harrison spluttered. "He's not even started school yet and you've got him solving algebraic equations?"

Clarke shook his head. "Oh, the basic stuff he got very quickly. He's onto quadratic formulae and measuring the gradients of tangents now."

The base of Harrison's empty glass rapped against the occasional table as he lowered it down. "Are you serious? Isn't that A-level stuff? For teenagers?"

"Ronnie says it's all a matter of just learning the methods," Charlie's mother beamed. "I think it's all very clever. I struggle to remember the method for making bread rolls."

I bet you'd forget the method to breathe if you were distracted by a Gucci handbag: Harrison mused inwardly. Outwardly, he said, "Shouldn't he be more into running around with a cardboard box on his head at his age? I know my two were. They spent six months talking to each other in duck-speak. The constant quacking drove me mad."

"He's never really been into all that infantile stuff," Clarke explained. "He was such a fast learner when it came to reading and was always asking about numbers. That's why we got him the nanny. She's been a great help."

"Oh, she's very good," Charlie's mum exclaimed in a deeply serious manner. "She's from Hungaria."

"Bulgaria, dear," Clarke corrected, patiently. "She's from Bulgaria."

Another stun bolt lacerated Harrison's brain as the blonde laughed at her own obvious stupidity. "Silly me! I always get it wrong. But, yes, she is very good. So efficient. I suppose they have to be over there. What with them being communists and all."

Clarke appeared somewhat uncomfortable as he shifted in his armchair. "Darling," he placed his hand on hers, "we've already had this conversation. They're not communists anymore. They're normal people. Just like you and me."

Heaven help the Hungarians: thought Harrison.

The pen glided fluidly over the paper. Letters danced with numbers and symbols that were completely alien to Hayley Clarke. She accepted that she had never been one of the high flyers at school but she appreciated beauty when she saw it. The fine cut of a Versace dress, the high polish of a pair of Dolce & Gabbana heels and the mathematical genius of her four-year-old son. Careful, so as not to crease her white, pristine dress, she knelt on the floor next to where Charlie was writing in his exercise book. To a distant onlooker he would look like any other pre-schooler doodling in a drawing book, but in reality...

In reality, what was it that her son was doing?

There were brackets, letters, large numbers, small numbers and all manner of symbols which looked like they belonged on a coat worn by Harry Potter rather than coming from the mind of a child.

Hayley smiled and fussed her son's hair.

He did not even blink. He just carried on writing.

The muffled sound of a foot on thick carpet caught her attention. She turned to face the young woman who had entered the room. "Oh, hello Anna." Hayley motioned to the large tumbler in the nanny's hand. "Is it lunch time already?"

"Yes, Mrs. Clarke. Charlie?"

The young boy looked up immediately.

"Time for your shake."

Quietly and with no protest, the young boy left his work and headed over to the broad, oak dining table where he sat and waited patiently as his nanny placed the tumbler on a coaster. "Drink it all up, now," the young woman instructed.

Charlie did as he was asked, silently gulping the thick drink down until the glass was empty and he was sporting a white moustache that he absent-mindedly removed with the back of his hand. After-wards, he slid off his chair and returned to his work.

"Anna?"

"Yes, Mrs. Clarke?"

"Can I ask what is actually in the shakes you give, Charlie?"

"Good things," the nanny replied as she carried the empty tumbler through to the kitchen. "Things to make him learn well."

"Darling?"

Ronald Clarke mumbled a vague response from his side of the bed.

"Do you think Charlie is happy?"

The grey-haired professor turned wearily onto his back. It had been a long day. Too many meetings and other things... He flinched at the memory and his hand absentmindedly rubbed his cheek. "Why shouldn't he be?"

"I don't know. It's just that when Mark came over the other day, I got the feeling he didn't approve, you know?"

Clarke sighed. "I can't say that I do."

His wife continued on with her train of thought, regardless: "And he's so quiet."

"Who? Mark Harrison?"

"No. Charlie. All he does is write out those sums in his book. All day long. I know it's all very clever and that, but is it normal?"

"Well, we know he's not normal by society's standards. He's a genius. We should be proud of that." Clarke turned back towards his soft pillow. It truly had been a long day. He wanted to go to sleep and forget all about it.

His wife apparently had other ideas.

"And then there's that stuff that Anna feeds him."

"You mean the shakes?" Clarke groaned into his pillow. "We've been over this before, Darling."

"Yes, yes, I know," Hayley flapped. "They're full of omega things to help his brain do what it needs to do. I know all that, but surely it wouldn't help to give him something else for a change?"

"Such as?"

"Oh, I don't know..." She tapped a manicured finger against her perfect lips. "Something fun. Something like a jam sandwich, perhaps?"

"So you want to fill him full of junk?"

"No..."

"Right then."

"But, those shakes... What's in them?"

"I told you..."

"Yes, I know. But what ingredients, exactly?"

Ronald Clarke realised that he did not really know.

"I told you, Mister Clarke, things to help him learn."

"Yes, I know that, Anna, but what exactly?"

The dark-haired nanny eyed her employer suspiciously. "You've never cared before. Why do you want to know now?"

"It's..." Clarke squirmed, "my wife that wants to know."

The nanny raised an eyebrow. "Oh, so today

you care about what she thinks, do you?" Acid dripped from her tongue. "Yesterday it was 'She means nothing to me,' and 'Marrying her was a mistake.' I think you need to decide what it is that you want from your life." She crossed her arms accusingly across her small bust.

Clarke flinched as he expected another slap, but none came. This was too much to endure. "This obviously isn't working," he muttered. "I think we will have to terminate your employment. I will pay you a month's wages but you have to be out of the house by the weekend."

He turned and scurried out of the room, his lover's eyes burning hatred into his back.

Hayley sipped from the hot cappuccino as she watched Charlie at the table. Gone were the maths books. Gone were the long numbers and funny-looking symbols. Instead, he had a large colouring book out in front of him and he was doodling with a pack of pencil crayons. From her spot on the sofa it looked like he was drawing a man of some sort. It was bright red with its arms out to its sides. Perhaps it was a cartoon character, a superhero of some type? That would explain the bright, vibrant scarlet.

Whatever it was, it was better than algebra.

Anna walked quietly into the room. "Mrs. Clarke."

The mother nodded at the nanny. In her hand, the brunette was holding a tumbler that was full to the brim with a bright red shake. Well, at least it looked unhealthy; that was a start, at least. Besides, the woman would be gone from their house in a few days and Hayley could start being a proper mother again, spoiling and pampering her little man.

She looked on as Anna gave the drink to Charlie and he glugged it down voraciously. "Wow, that must be really tasty. What's in it?"

The nanny removed the empty tumbler and gently ran her fingers through the young boy's hair. "Something to make him happy," she said. "Something to make him happy."

Hayley woke with a start. She had been dreaming. It had been such a sweet dream too. Ronnie and she had been walking along a deserted beach with Charlie. The three of them had been hand-in-hand and smiling contentedly. She had been wearing a long, white flowing dress and her feet had felt warm in the sand. The sea had been shushing against the shore and dolphins had been diving in and out of the surf.

An idyllic paradise.

Then there had been lightning and thunder. A massive clap had shot out through the air and she had woken in a panic.

Her heart pounded as she sat bolt upright in bed, her eyes wide open and her hair plastered to her scalp.

The light was on.

Why was the light on?

Ronnie was stirring next to her as she turned and saw that they were not alone. Charlie was stood at the foot of the bed in his nightwear.

"Sweetie?" she asked. "What's the matter?"

Her son stood silent in his brown, checked

pyjamas his eyes off in some middle distance.

"He's sleepwalking," Ronald grumbled, slipping his glasses on and peering over the tops of them as he always did. "God knows why."

Hayley slipped out of the bed and went over to her son. Gently, she slipped her arm around his shoulders. "Come on, sweetie. Let's get you back to bed." Silently, Charlie did as he was told and followed his mother back to his bedroom. Hayley gave a small gasp when she opened the door. There were drawings everywhere. Reams and reams of sketches and doodles. All of them pictures of people or parts of people in vibrant red crayon. She stooped down and picked one up then wished that she had not. It was the inside of someone's head: the muscle, tissue and fibre.

"Oh, Charlie!" she cried. "No wonder you were having nightmares." Carefully she led him to his bed, lifted him up and tucked him in. When she was sure that he was soundly asleep she scooped up all the sketches and marched back to her bedroom.

"Ronnie! Have you seen these?" Hayley demanded, thrusting the pictures under her husband's nose. "What the hell is going on?"

Clarke leafed through the images and shrugged. "So he has a thing about anatomy? What's the problem?"

All Hayley could do was stare at her husband, dumbfounded.

"At least it's not maths," Clarke grumbled and, dropping the pictures to the floor, settled back down to sleep.

Hayley lay awake listening to every noise in the house. There was the scratching of the tree against the window, the creaking of their bed as her husband shifted in his sleep, the ticking of the bedside clock. The list was endless. It was an unwelcome symphony of music being played with extreme vigour by an unseen orchestra intent on keeping her from her sleep.

She tried burying her head in her pillow.

She tried going to sleep with her arms crossed over her ears.

Nothing worked so she just lay there and listened. Listened to the scratch, the creak, the tick.

Scratch, creak, tick,

Scratch, creak, tick,

Scratch, creak, thud, tick.

Hayley held her breath and listened again. There had been another noise, a rogue instrument in the nocturnal orchestration. She peered over at Ronald. He was sound asleep and she was sure that he would be none too pleased if she woke him again.

With as much stealth as she could manage, she swung her legs out of the warm bed and made her way to the door. Cautiously, she peered down the landing.

Nothing moved in the shadows.

There came another thud. It was downstairs.

Hayley glanced back nervously into the bedroom. She could wake Ronald. She could ring the police. She could do any number of things but she would be overreacting. Instead, she cautiously made her way along the dark landing. Her hand hovered momentarily over the light switch then drew back. What if it was an intruder? A light would draw them to her.

She edged down the stairs in darkness.

At first, everything seemed as she had left it when she had gone up to bed. The front door was closed and the curtains were drawn. Nothing out of the norm.

The living room door, however, was open.

Had she shut it?

Perhaps she had left it open?

Hayley could not remember.

She crept away from the bottom stair and padded over to the door in her bare feet, her short nightie brushing against her thighs. Suddenly she felt cold and exposed. A shiver ran down her spine.

As she carefully made her way into the living room, she became aware of the notion that she was not alone. There was a light noise from behind the sofa. Her heart rising up in her throat, she crept as stealthily as she could towards the sofa, the thick pile of the carpet pressing up between her bare toes. The woman held her breath tighter than she had ever held her handbag on a crowded bus and her heart felt like it was going to pound out of her chest. Every instinct was telling her to turn and flee but she had to know what was down here, what was hiding.

Slowly, tentatively, the thick pile masking the sound of her hesitant footsteps, Hayley ventured around to the rear of the sofa, her eyes starting to become accustomed to the gloom and the varying depths of the shadows. The tension she felt knotting up inside her was unbearable; it was as if she had been trussed up in an over-tight corset, unable to free herself.

One hand steadying herself on the top of the sofa, she peered around its back.

There was nothing there.

Absolutely nothing.

Hayley let out an immense groan and breathed in sweet relief as she sank back against the finely upholstered piece of furniture. It was okay. Everything was okay. It had just been her imagination.

She shrieked in pain as something sharp dug into her ankle.

Looking down she saw a knife sticking out from under the sofa, clutched in a small hand.

Hayley turned to run but her foot would not move properly. As she twisted and fell she could only watch in disbelief as her small son crawled out from between the legs of the sofa.

Anna flicked on the lights and let a feeling of satisfaction draw a smile to her lips. Charlie was sat slumped over a stack of drawings that lay strewn around the dining table. The nanny tiptoed over and slowly stroked his hair as she carefully leafed through the perfectly articulated sketches of human anatomy. Her finger traced the ventricles of a heart, the workings of a lower intestine and the musculature of dissected torsos – male and female.

She nodded with approval. He had been most meticulous; there was not a drop of blood on any of the drawings.

The same could not be said for the rest of the

house.

Carefully, lovingly, she scooped the young genius up in her arms and carried him out to her waiting car.

First Hunt – Then

The small fire crackled in the hollow pit that had been roughly dug in the rocky floor of the small cave. The boy shivered as he rubbed his hands together in a vain attempt to draw some heat from the puny flames that danced languidly in the cold night air. He glanced over at the tall silhouette that was framed in the opening to the cave.

No shivers over there.

No sign of discomfort whatsoever.

The dark form just stood, a black statue looking out over the scrub and the surrounding plains. What was it watching? The boy had no idea, nor did he care. Right now he cared about just one thing.

His stomach rumbled loudly.

The silhouette moved as the figure turned to regard the boy. "Are you hungry?" it asked.

The boy nodded. "Yes. Thirsty too."

"When did you last eat?" The voice was deep and dry like a sandstorm rushing in from a distance ready to consume an unsuspecting village.

The boy trembled. "When you gave me an apple."

The figure cocked its head to one side. "Was that not two days ago?"

The boy nodded vigorously.

"Why have you not eaten since?" asked the voice, truly perplexed.

"I was afraid to ask."

The silhouette broke form as the man (if the boy could call him that) bent down towards the youngster. The flames of the fire flickered warmly in his worried eyes. "Never be afraid of me. I would never, ever harm you. Understand?"

The boy nodded once more. He felt the churning of dread in the pit of his stomach settle down as something akin to an emotional blanket swathed his tired body. He smiled up into the eyes of his saviour, the one who had whisked him away from a life of destitution and poverty to one of...

Well, he was not sure what yet but he knew it would be better than it had been.

The man smiled back at him. "Let's go find you something to eat."

The man that was not a man cursed himself in the silence of his mind: Stupid. Stupid. Stupid. How could he have been so forgetful? Had it really been two days since he had eradicated the Construct vermin in the town of Salem? He sighed. His concept of time and mortal matters was becoming somewhat less than tangible with every day.

Perhaps that was why he had let the boy come with him? He was a tenuous grasp on day-to-day reality.

He looked down at the small chap. How old was he? Ten? Eleven? He was so malnourished; it was hard to tell. His tattered clothes hung on him like rags and his bare feet scuffed the dust as they walked out onto the plains.

The creature that looked like a man but whose heart did not beat and lungs did not breathe suddenly found himself somewhere else. A happier time where another young boy skipped idly beside him, carrying over his shoulder a fishing rod that was longer than he was tall. They were off to catch some fish for their supper from the creek near their house. The boy's mother was at home setting the table and preparing water with which to cook their meal.

"What's wrong?"

The boy of now spoke and dragged the man that was not a man back to the present.

"Nothing."

The boy pointed upwards. "You have something on your face."

He rubbed the heel of his hand against his cheek and it came away smeared red with the blood of a single tear. "It's nothing," he reassured his young companion. "Nothing at all." He took the family snapshot, the final moment before his world had died, and locked it up securely in the strongbox of his subconscious. "So have you ever been hunting before?"

The boy shook his head. "No, Sir. My dad thought I was too young."

"Really?" The man raised an eyebrow and muttered something quietly about modern youth being treated as soft as a whore's caress. "So you've never fired a gun?"

The boy shook his head as a heavy killing machine was pressed into his small hand.

"It's easy," came the abridged explanation. "Point that end at the thing you wish to eat and pull the trigger."

"Wh...what if I miss?"

"You go hungry."

He watched the boy hold the pistol as if it were going to turn around and bite him then sighed deeply. "Perhaps we ought to try using a snare instead?"

Half an hour later, the two hunters were skulking behind a small, scrub-covered mound that overlooked a snare set carefully where the older of the two knew a rabbit would run. His sharp eyes could see small disturbances in the dusty ground that had been caused by the scampering of rabbits and his nose could smell the scent of at least two lingering lagomorphs. He crouched quietly under the night sky, his limbs unaffected by the need to remain motionless and still.

Next to him, the boy fidgeted.

He ignored the disturbance.

The boy fidgeted again.

Still he ignored it.

The boy coughed.

Without moving his eyes from the rabbit run, the man said, "Do you really want to eat?"

"My legs ache."

"Worse than your stomach?"

"No."

"Then ignore them."

Quietly, the boy shifted position until he was lying on his front, peering through the scrub. "So how does it work, again?"

"The rabbit bounces happily through the thicket as it usually does; the wire catches around its neck and kills it."

"Kills it?"

"Yes."

"How?"

"It restricts the flow of blood to the brain and the rabbit suffocates."

The boy leaned back and looked aghast at his teacher. "That's awful! It's so cruel!"

"Keep your voice down," the man hissed. "You'll startle the rabbits."

"And that's worse than throttling them?"

"It is if you want to fill that bottomless pit of yours."

The boy sank down against the small hillock and folded his arms across his chest. "Well, I don't like it," he pouted.

The man let his face sink into the dusty earth. Was this what eternity had planned for him? "Do you like being hungry more?" he snapped then immediately regretted the harshness of his tone when he lifted his head and saw the boy's face crumple. "Oh, no. Wait. I'm sorry... I didn't mean to..." His voice faltered as the young lad threw himself into his arms and sobbed.

They had given up on rabbit. By the time that

the boy had gained control of his emotions the fluffy meals had long since scarpered. Instead, they had decided to make their way to the next town. The boy did not know what its name was but he knew that it was not too far. His late father had taken him there for supplies a few times when he was younger.

As they walked along the dusty track the boy appeared to be pondering something.

"What's on your mind, Son?"

"What's your name?"

The man raised an eyebrow without even breaking stride. He had been expecting this question sooner or later, this one and another.

He did not want to have to answer the other one just yet.

"Justice."

"Is it biblical?"

"Pardon?"

"My dad used to say that names oughta be biblical or they weren't proper names."

"Well, there's lots of justice in the Bible."

"Why did your folks choose it?"

"They didn't. I did."

The boy stopped in his tracks. Justice carried on walking, feeling the subtle change in air patterns as the boy's mouth hung open in shock. "You chose your own name?"

"Yes. When I started out doing what I do."

There was the scampering of bare feet as the boy caught up with him. "You mean like killing bad'uns?"

"You could put it like that."

They walked in silence for a while. Justice

could see the lights of the next settlement start to glow on the horizon. They would be there within the hour and then he would find food for the boy.

"What was he? Carson, I mean."

Justice considered his answer carefully. How to explain a war that had been waged in the shadows for as long as his kind could remember? How to tell this boy that everything he believed in was built upon a misconception that humans were the only sentient creatures that walked the planet.

"He was a monster. A terrible monster."

"What are you?"

What resembled Justice's heart trembled as the boy asked the question that he had not wanted to answer just yet.

"I'm a different kind of monster."

The boy thought that Stuartsville was more or less the same layout as Salem: a high street with a saloon that doubled up as a hotel, a store with a hitching post outside, a sheriff's office and a few buildings that he could not identify in the dark. He followed Justice over to the saloon. The clock tower above the sheriff's office read just short of ten o'clock so the sound of music and revelry could still be clearly heard sauntering its way out of the double swing doors.

"We'll lodge here and get you fed," the man who called himself a monster said matter-of-factly as he climbed the few stairs to the doors. The boy followed him, the wood feeling worn under his bare feet. He entered the saloon behind his companion and the doors swung shut behind them.

Silence descended as all eyes turned towards the tall stranger with the child.

The boy tugged at Justice's long coat and the man peered down at him. "Do you always have that effect?" the boy asked in a loud whisper.

There was the sound of a feminine chuckle followed by a cough and the awkward silence was broken causing the background bar room noise to resume.

"It has been known," Justice smiled. "Sit yourself down here." He pulled a chair from under a table for the boy. "I'll get us a room."

As his companion's boots thunked their way across the floor to the bar, the boy surveyed his surroundings. The saloon seemed to contain all manner of folk, most of them sat with their friends enjoying a drink at the end of the day. On one table he saw a very pretty lady running her fingers up the chest of a man who must have been her father judging by the age of him, although why he had his arm around her in such a fashion, the boy could not tell. He spied an elderly couple at another table. The woman had a touch of grey hair protruding from under her white bonnet and she sat knitting whilst her bowler-hatted spouse drank carefully so as not to get whiskey in a voluminous moustache that reminded the boy of a pair of horse tails.

The boy's eyes stopped when they reached the next table. There sat three men with whom he did not think he would wish to mix. They wore rough, dusty clothes and scowls that spoke of ill intent. Also, their eyes never left Justice's back as he spoke to the landlord before turning and beckoning the boy over. "We have a room," he explained as he led the way upstairs. "It sounds basic but it should suffice. The owner will bring some food up shortly."

When they reached the top of the stairs to the landing that overlooked the bar, the boy said, "Those men were watching you."

Justice glanced out across the bar and breathed in deeply.

For a moment he stood stock still, just as he had earlier in the cave mouth, then he turned and continued along to their room. He opened the door and stood aside for the boy to enter. "Wait in here. Your food will come along presently," he instructed and made to leave.

"Where are you going?"

"I have business to attend to," the gunslinger explained and shut the door.

The boy lay back on the huge bed and belched loudly. On the tray next to him lay the carcass of a chicken, a few crumbs of bread and an empty glass. He felt as if he had eaten like a king! His belly was stretched and full, somewhat uncomfortably so. He rolled off the bed, stretched and padded around the bedroom in an attempt to aid his digestion. As he did so, he wondered where Justice had gotten to. He glanced out of the window and the clock tower told him that it had just gone midnight.

Had two hours really passed?

The onset of worry started to gnaw where the food lay in his stomach. Surely Justice should be back by now? The boy trotted over to the door and peeked out. The bar was in darkness; not a soul moved about downstairs and the lighting had been extinguished. Carefully, so as not to disturb any other residents, the boy tiptoed along the landing and down the stairs before heading over to the front doors. He pushed one aside and looked out into the street. As he did so, he saw the three rough-looking men turning around a corner and down an alley. He remembered the way that they had watched Justice from their table and the manner in which the gunslinger had scented the room.

Were they the same monsters like Carson?

Was Justice in trouble?

The boy made up his mind to find out and followed them, silently.

The clock tower read quarter past the hour as Justice re-entered the saloon in a foul mood. The Constructs had eluded him. He had gone back down into the bar and sat waiting until they had left before following them out into his realm, the night. Then, as he had quietly stalked them through the dark, something had distracted him. There had been the softest of whispers and a new scent had drifted over on the still, night air. He had stood enrapt as the smell had danced inside his nostrils and fired off certain synapses in his brain.

It had felt familiar yet new. It reminded him of a scent from the past yet was inherently different.

The hunter had shaken his head in an attempt to clear his wandering thoughts before turning and realising that his prey had vanished. Cursing silently, he had hunted in vain through the alleys of the town but had been unable to pick up the sickening smell that marked them for what they were; the new, intruding fragrance occupied his olfactory senses, blinding his senses to the task at hand.

In the end he had given up and returned to the saloon. Stomping disconsolately into his room, he saw just the empty bed and the remains of the devoured supper. His eyes darted round hunting for clues before he turned and ran back out faster than the human eye could observe, images from his former life rising up to haunt him once more.

The first inkling that there had been something wrong was the smell of woodsmoke, next was the drifting clouds of black that rose over the hill from their house. He had told his son to wait in the trees where it was safe whilst he ran as fast as his mortal legs could manage back to the furnace that had once been his home. Inarticulate words had gorged their way out of his throat when he saw the lifeless body of his beautiful wife discarded on the path to their once quiet paradise. Then there had been the shrieks of fear as he had turned and seen his son being dragged out of the trees by a steel-eyed beast dressed in furs and leather.

"This brat yours?" the stranger had yelled. "Screams louder that his momma!" Then, in one swift movement he had thrown the boy the floor and pumped two bullets in the child's head.

The man that used to be had just stood still, unable to move as the shadowy horrors of a cruel world had torn his sanctuary apart. Even when the cur had raised the gun towards him he had been unable to turn and flee. Instead, he had slumped to the floor as the side of his head had exploded in agony and darkness had closed around him.

When his eyes had reopened it had been to a whole new world. A world where his senses were heightened enabling him to achieve three important tasks:

Find the Eternals.

Protect the Twins.

Await the Divergence.

Right now, however, he was depending on these same senses to perform just one task: find the boy before the Constructs did.

"Hello, Sonny," came the elderly voice. "Are you lost?"

The boy sat on a crate with his head in his hands. Some tracker he was. Within a few minutes he had lost his prey. The three rough-looking men had vanished around a corner and he had no idea where they had gone so he had sat himself down to work out his next move.

Then the elderly couple from the saloon had wandered down the alley.

"No, Ma'am," he said to the old woman in the white bonnet, "I'm just collecting my thoughts."

"In an alley?" the old man chuckled from behind his horse tail moustache. "Surely that's not a good idea at this time of night? There could be all sorts about."

"I'll be fine," the boy assured them. "I have a protector."

The elderly couple gave each other a curious look. "You mean that tall fellow you were with earlier?" asked the woman.

The boy nodded confidently.

"Funny," said the old man, his voice sounding suddenly rheumy and wet as if he had a throat full of phlegm, "but I don't see the vampire anywhere near right now."

Hairs rose on the back of the boy's neck as he slowly slid off the crate. "What did you say?" he began to ask, but the words hung quivering on his tongue as he watched stunned whilst the skin of the two old-timers started to ripple and flex under their clothes. The old man's moustache was sucked back into his face as his features sunk into a thick, brown substance that bore just a gash where his mouth should be. The woman's appearance followed suit and they lumbered towards him, their clothes sloughing off their clammy bodies to the floor.

The boy tried to run; he really did, but his feet just did not seem to want to move. Monsters: he thought to himself. These were the monsters. Not those men. Then the wet hand of the thing that used to be a sweet, old lady that sat in saloons knitting clothes from homespun yarn clasped the youth on the shoulder and dragged him towards her ragged mouth. He squirmed at the sight of the putrid-smelling liquid trickling from the slavering orifice. It stank like a stagnant pond at the height of summer and made the boy feel like retching, but even that was not possible as fear constricted every muscle in his body.

He was aware of a deep rattling emanating from the mouth of the thing that used to be a man and realised that it was laughing, enjoying watching this young human paralysed with fear.

Then there was a noise that sounded like a boot wrenching itself out of mud and the laughing abruptly halted mid-chuckle. The boy's paralysis broke and he turned to see the monster that used to be an old man slump to the floor in two parts. Next to him stood a pretty young woman dressed in a frock coat and a small hat. In her hand was a bright, gleaming sword.

She pulled back her lips in a smile and the boy saw the sharpest teeth he could ever have imagined. In an instant she was a blur and the thing that used to be an old woman was no longer holding his hand. The well-dressed woman had the creature pinned against a wall and had plunged her teeth into its neck. There was a wet warbling noise as the thing tried to free itself but eventually the scream sounded raspy and dry as the monster turned to dust in the younger woman's embrace.

The boy heard the sound of footsteps behind him and turned to see another stranger. This one was a man, and what a man! He stood taller than Justice and his hair was a mane of bright yellow. Muscles rippled under his travelling coat as he lifted the severed remains of the other creature in his hands and rapidly drained them dry.

Just as he was becoming accustomed to the appearance of his apparent saviours, the boy felt a rush of wind and found himself whisked up into the arms of Justice. He looked up and saw relief in his companion's eyes before they tracked across the alley to the blonde giant and filled with awe.

He set the boy on the alley floor and sank down onto one knee.

"Your Majesty," said the gunslinger

The blonde man walked over with regal confidence and, taking Justice by the arm, lifted him from his genuflection.

"My son and heir," said the king, unadulterated love filling the words as he turned him to face the young woman. "Let me introduce you to your new sister."

The woman smiled prettily, her blue eyes twinkling in the night, and held out her hand.

"Hello," she said. "My name is Nightingale."

Author's Notes

Well, I hope you enjoyed those little tales of horror and fantasy. As with my previous outing into short story land, Oh Taste And See, I just want to take a few minutes to say a few words about the stories that you have just read.

Relic.

As with a lot of what I write, this story was based on a real event — not the escalating apocalypse but the painting of a car in a back alley. I used to have an old, temperamental Ford Fiesta which kept getting rusty under the radiator, so one day I took a tin of gloss paint and went at it hammer and tongs. The result was a shiny white finish on the car but various indelible splatters on the cobbles. I could have cleaned them off but I was already covered in the sticky gloop of white paint. As a result I left the mess alone and there it remains to this day. Hopefully no-one will ever dig the cobbles up.

Test Flight.

In Oh Taste And See I included the hundred word piece Extraction. I enjoyed the challenge of creating such a short piece so much that I decided to have another go. I feel that the compact nature of the story suits quirky, little tales. I hope that you do too.

Second Time Around.

As I have mentioned before in various places, the fallen angel Asherah is one of my favourite characters. The ultimate femme fatale who can turn a collection of the dullest bank managers or accountants into the most fervent of fanatical acolytes just by the humming of a simple tune is a character who will appear time and time again in my ever expanding universe. She is already scheduled to reappear in a number of future Sam Spallucci books, a forthcoming novel regarding the fall of Troy, my magnus opus Fallen Angel and ultimately, after the Divergence has swept across the universe, we shall see her and her longtime companion Asmodeus riding side by side in the service of the mysterious Kanor (sorry — spoilers). So I thought it only right that you had the chance to see the her first appearances (The Case Of The Fastidious Phantom and Sam Spallucci: Ghosts From The Past) from her point of view.

Needs Must.

I have to say that, at the time of writing, this is my personal favourite of my shorts stories to date. I wanted to create a monster with whom the reader could sympathise and come to love then pull the metaphorical rug out from under their feet right at the end. I am great fan of the Universal Frankenstein movies as well as Mel Brooks' Young Frankenstein. In both movies, the scene with the little girl always sticks in my head. The story of Odd Bod and Emily is my little homage to that.

You might be interested to know that there is a video of me reading an extract from this story which I have posted on my YouTube channel. Look for "A.S.Chambers' 2014 Christmas Rambling".

Just Like Everybody Else.

I have very little to say about this piece apart from the fact that you know it is true.

Prodigy.

This story was the product of two things. The first was a long coffee on a wet, windy autumn morning. I was stranded inside a coffee shop, hiding from the weather and started to doodle on a napkin. Ten minutes later I had sketched the plot for Prodigy. I still have the napkin somewhere. The second was a book that I was reading when I started to write All Things Dark And Dangerous. I am a great fan of the science fiction writer Philip K. Dick and I love the way that his approach to writing makes reality seem somewhat stilted and dull with something lurking underneath. In the book Paycheck there is a short story entitled Nanny about robot nannies that go out and battle at night. I fell in love with this tale and Dick's style so, when I started to pen Prodigy, I decided to follow his lead and take that dull, mundane lifestyle then flip it over to see what horror lurked underneath.

First Hunt (Now & Then).

I love vampires. I have done ever since I read Dracula back in my dim, distant teenage years. I find the thought that there are these creatures of the night lurking in the shadows of our lives to be both enticing and terrifying. So it is that I am currently building up to a major vampire novel which I hope to release in 2016. Sam Spallucci: Dark Justice will see the Children of Cain return to Lancaster on the trail of both Constructs and a renegade from their ranks. The six vampire stories regarding Nightingale and Justice from Oh Taste And See, All Things Dark And Dangerous and next year's short story collection Let All Mortal Flesh will take the reader along on the build up to this tale of vampiric honour, bloodlust and revenge. I hope that you enjoy the journey.

So, there you have it, just a few notes about my latest batch of stories. I hope that you will join me again with my next book Sam Spallucci: Shadows Of Lancaster when we see Lancaster gripped in the heat of a witch hunt.

If you have enjoyed my stories and want to know more about me and my work, then please look me up on Facebook, Twitter and all the other usual places. The details of these and my website are at the back of this book.

Also, could you please take a few minutes to leave some favourable words on Amazon and

Goodreads? It is always heartening to get feedback from you, my readers.

All the best,
ASC

About The Author

A.S.Chambers resides in Lancaster, England. He lives a fairly simple life of walking in the countryside, gazing at mountains and wondering if clouds taste of candy-floss.

He is quite happy for, and in fact would encourage, you to follow him on Facebook, Instagram X, TikTok, Patreon and YouTube.

There is also a nice, shiny website:
www.aschambers.co.uk

Milton Keynes UK
Ingram Content Group UK Ltd.
UKHW041131030624
443552UK00001B/14

9 781915 679451